Copyright © 2021 Kira Parris-Moore

All rights reserved. Published by Books2Inspire. BOOKS2INSPIRE and associated logos and trademarks and/or registered trademarks of Books2Inspire.

No part of this book may be used or reproduced in any manner whatsoever without written permission except in the case of brief quotations embodied in critical articles and reviews.

For information regarding permission, email books2inspireu@gmail.com. Visit us on the web at www.books2inspire.com

Published in: Durham, NC USA.
Library of Congress Control Number: 9781734437492.
Parris-Moore, Kira (2021). Trey the Chef: Cooking Camp (Kira Parris-Moore). Durham: Books2Inspire.
ISBN: 978-1-7344374-9-2.
Printed in the United States of America.

Trey the Chef: Cooking Camp

Kira Parris-Moore
Illustrated by
Emily Zieroth

This book is dedicated to my two boys, Trey and Kam. You both are the lights of my life and I feel blessed to have you as my children. I also dedicate this book to my supportive husband CJ. Your unwavering support means more to me than you will ever know.

~KPM

Perfect my technique.
Learn some new tricks.
Make sure my dishes get first pick!

My teacher tells the class, "He is overwhelmed. Give him some time so he can settle in."

She then bends down to talk to me, reassures me that it will be okay, just take as much time as I need.

The teacher comes over, a smile on her face. She says to the class, "Oooooooh! Look at what Trey has made!"

The kids in class just stare at me,
Like I am some sort of weird discovery.
One by one they ask me, "Can you help me with my dish?" They tell me cooking like me would be their biggest wish.

Before the day has come to an end, I can't believe I have made so many friends!
They say they are surprised that someone like me could make something so amazing and tasty!

When I see my parents after class, I tell them
the good news!

They say that they are not surprised
and always knew.

"Trey you are who you are.
But despite your challenges,
you will go very far.
One day soon,
you will become something big.
Bigger than we ever imagined."

I smile that night, knowing no dream is too big.
For anyone, not even this little kid.

I will work hard and someday I will hear them say, "Nice to meet you, Master Chef Trey!"

The End.

Recipes

Trey has friends all over the United States that wanted to help him out and share some their recipes with the world. We hope you enjoy these tasty dishes because cooking and eating with friends is so much fun!

Olivia's Homemade Unicorn Ice Cream

Ingredients:

- 1 14 oz can of sweetened condensed milk
- 1 pint of heavy cream
- 1 teaspoon of vanilla extract
- Purple, pink, blue, and yellow gel icing color

Directions:

1) Pour entire pint of heavy cream into the bowl of a stand mixer or use a handheld mixer.
2) Mix on medium high for 1 to 2 minutes until cream stiffens and peaks form.
3) Pour entire can of sweetened condensed milk into the heavy cream and stir until completely mixed.
4) Separate equal amounts of mixture into 4 bowls.
5) Add a small amount of each color to its own mixture bowl. Stir until desired color is reached.
6) Layer each color mixture in a clean and dry bowl or jar in any order you like.
7) Cover tightly and place in freezer for 8 hours or overnight.
8) Take out of freezer and let sit at room temperature for 3 to 5 minutes when you are ready to eat it.
9) Enjoy!

King's Banana Split Roll-Ups

Ingredients:

- Ready-to-use Crepes (two per person)
- 1 tbsp Hazelnut-cocoa spread
- 1 Fresh Banana
- 1 Can of Diced Pineapples
- 1/4 of Fresh Sliced Strawberries
- 1 to 3 Maraschino jarred Cherries
- 1 dollop of Whipped Cream

Directions:

1) Slice bananas and strawberries with a butterknife, set aside.

2) Stack two crepes, one on top of the other, on a large plate. (Crepes are very thin. Using two keeps the roll-up from falling apart.)

3) With a spoon or butterknife, smooth hazelnut spread onto one-half of the crepe.

4) Add a few banana slices on top of the hazelnut spread.

5) Layer sliced strawberries on top of the bananas.

6) Layer diced pineapples on top of the strawberries.

7) Add a cherry (or two or three!)

8) When you've finished layering the fruit, turn the plate so that the fruity, chocolate-covered half is on top.

9) Lifting from the top, gently and carefully roll the crepe toward you until secure.

10) Cut the roll-up in half.

11) Garnish with whipped cream and a cherry.

12) ENJOY!

Brianne's Savory Plantain Pancakes

Ingredients:

Serves: 2
2 tablespoons of olive oil
1 large, very ripe plantain
¼ cup scallions, chopped
2 egg whites
1 whole egg
½ tsp garlic powder
½ tsp cumin powder
¼ tsp chili powder
Salt & pepper to taste

Directions:

1) Heat oil in a large frying pan or griddle on medium heat.

2) In a small bowl, mash the plantain with a fork until smooth and add the scallions.

3) In a large bowl, mix an egg and egg whites.

4) Then and add garlic, cumin, chili, and salt & pepper to taste.

5) Pour plantain and onion into the egg mixture and mix with a fork till combined (Blend in blender for an extra smooth consistency).

6) Take 2 tablespoons of the batter and place on the hot pan—flip pancakes with a spatula for 10 to 15 seconds on each side or until you see craters in the batter.

7) Enjoy!

Katie's Whole Grain Jam Surprise Muffins

Made with oats and whole wheat, these muffins are a filling and fun breakfast to get you through a busy morning. Choose your favorite jam to fill the muffins, or use a few different kinds for a yummy surprise!

Ingredients:

3/4 cup butter
3/4 cup rolled oats
1/2 cup all-purpose flour
1/2 cup whole-wheat flour
1/4 teaspoon baking soda
1/3 cup brown sugar, packed
1 cup buttermilk
1 large egg
1 teaspoon vanilla extract
1/3 cup jam or jelly of your choice
(I like to use peach or strawberry jam or orange marmalade)

Directions:

1) Preheat the oven to 350ºF and line a 12-cup muffin pan with paper muffin liners.
2) Have an adult help you melt the butter in a heat-proof mixing bowl or measuring cup and then cool the melted butter in the fridge for a few minutes. In a large mixing bowl, stir together the oats, all-purpose flour, whole-wheat flour, and baking soda until they are well mixed.
3) Remove the cooled butter from the fridge and add the brown sugar, whisking to combine them well. Add the buttermilk, egg, and vanilla extract to the butter mixture and whisk until combined. Pour the wet ingredients into the oat and flour mixture and use a wooden spoon or spatula to fold the ingredients together until the batter is just combined. If you stir too long or too hard, the batter might be a little tough, so try to just stir enough to get the flour moistened.
4) Fill each paper muffin liner about 1/2 full of batter. Using the back of a spoon, or a clean finger, create a little well in the center of each batter-filled cup. Place about ½ tbsp of jam or jelly in each well, then cover the jelly with enough batter to fill each muffin cup about ¾ full.
5) With an adult's help, place the muffins in the preheated oven. Set the timer for 15 minutes. After 15 minutes, check the muffins by sticking a toothpick into one of the muffins in the middle of the pan. If there is some wet looking batter sticking to the toothpick, bake the muffins for another 5 minutes and then check them again. If the toothpick looks dry or just has a few crumbs sticking to it, the muffins are done! Carefully remove the muffins from the oven and let them cool in the pan for at least 10 minutes before removing them from the pan. Enjoy!

Gregory's Tasty Squash Pasta

Ingredients:

- 1 spaghetti squash, scrubbed with clean vegetable brush under running water
- 1 red bell pepper, scrubbed with clean vegetable brush under running water and diced
- 1/2 sweet onion, scrubbed with clean vegetable brush under running water and diced
- 2 1/2 Tbsp olive oil
- 1/2 tsp salt
- 1/2 tsp garlic powder
- 1 shallot, gently rubbed under cold running water and finely diced
- 2 lemons, scrubbed with clean vegetable brush under running water, cut in half, and juiced
- 4 oz grated parmesan cheese
- 6 large basil leaves, gently rub under cold running water and finely diced

Directions:

1) Wash hands thoroughly with soap and water.
2) Cut the spaghetti squash in half, remove the seeds, and then place in the microwave for 6-8 minutes, or until tender.
3) Once the squash is tender, remove from the microwave and allow to cool. Once cooled, scrape the squash with a fork to make the "spaghetti". Set to the side.
4) Add 1/2 Tbsp of olive oil to a large sauté pan on medium-high heat, and then add the diced bell pepper and onion. Continue to stir, and then add 1/4 tsp salt and 1/4 tsp garlic powder. Cook until tender, for about 5 minutes, then add the spaghetti

squash pasta.

5) Meanwhile, to make the sauce, combine the diced shallot, lemon juice, 2 Tbsp olive oil, 1/4 tsp salt, and 1/4 tsp garlic powder in a small bowl. Then, add the sauce to the pan with the pasta and veggies. Stir until well incorporated.
6) Remove from heat and stir in the parmesan cheese and finely diced basil. Enjoy!

Resources for people with autism

Disclaimer: This is a list that the author has compiled through active research. The author does not endorse any of these resources and this list is offered for informational purposes ONLY. The author does not take any responsibility for any resources that may be unsatisfactory that are included in this list. In addition, this list is not a comprehensive list and should not be treated as such.

1) National Autistic Society- https://www.autism.org.uk/
2) US Autism Association: https://www.usautism.org/
3) Autistic Self Advocacy- https://autisticadvocacy.org/
4) Autism Society- https://www.autism-society.org/
5) Autism Now- https://autismnow.org/
6) Organization for Autism Research- https://researchautism.org/
7) Autism Research Institute- https://www.autism.org/
8) Autism Science Foundation- https://autismsciencefoundation.org/
9) Autism National Committee- https://www.autcom.org/
10) Center for Autism & Related Disorders- https://www.centerforautism.com/
11) American Academy of Pediatrics: Autism- https://services.aap.org/en/community/aap-councils/council-on-children-with-disabilities/
12) Asperger/Autism Network: https://www.aane.org/
13) Brain and Behavior Research Foundation: https://www.bbrfoundation.org/research/autism
14) Color of Autism- https://www.thecolorofautism.org/
15) Grupo Salto- https://gruposalto.org/ (in Spanish)
16) Autism Grown Up: https://www.autismgrownup.com/
17) National Autism Associate: https://nationalautismassociation.org/
18) Southwest Austism Research and Resource Center: https://www.autismcenter.org/
19) International Society for Autism Research: https://www.autism-insar.org/default.aspx

Meet the Author!!

Kira is an autism mom, licensed therapist, and author of several children's books including Trey the Chef, Suzy the Dressmaker, and Carrie the Photographer. Kira considers herself to be a mental health and disabilities advocate who believes that early intervention with children offers the best prognosis. Kira hopes that her literature will be the catalyst to help children further their emotional intelligence by recognizing and appreciating the differences between them and other children creating a more tolerant world in the future.

Meet the Illustrator

 Emily Zieroth is a Canadian, self-taught artist that has been illustrating children's books for over a decade. It has become a true passion of her's and the thought that kids from around the world smile at the illustrations she has drawn brings such a joy to her life. With every book comes a new adventure and a new chance to learn and grow. She hopes that she is able to portray her love for her work with every story that she illustrates for.

CPSIA information can be obtained
at www.ICGtesting.com
Printed in the USA
BVHW051305310521
PP12299700001B/1